"Bone-shakingly scary!"

"Genuinely funny and genuinely sp-sp-spooky,
Tommy Donbavand's Scream Street puts
humorous horror firmly on the map!"

Philip Ardagh

"Lightning-paced, bloodcurdling fun. I wish I'd
been able to visit Scream Street as a kid!"

Darren Shan

"Exactly the sort of grisly, gross and
hilarious stuff that kids will love!"

Eoin Colfer

"Like Harry Potter with extra bite,
Scream Street is fast-moving and scary –
but it has a big heart (which it
keeps in the fridge, of course!)."

Philip Reeve

"A great read with some
great characters!"

David Melling

SCREAM STREET

SECRET OF THE CHANGELING

TOMMY DONBAVAND

WALKER BOOKS

This is a work of fiction. Names, characters, places and incidents are
either the product of the author's imagination or, if real, are used fictitiously.

First published 2011 by Walker Books Ltd
87 Vauxhall Walk, London SE11 5HJ

2 4 6 8 10 9 7 5 3

Text © 2011 Tommy Donbavand
Illustrations © 2011 Cartoon Saloon Ltd

The right of Tommy Donbavand to be identified
as author of this work has been asserted by him in accordance
with the Copyright, Designs and Patents Act 1988

This book has been typeset in Bembo Educational

Printed and bound in Great Britain by Clays Ltd, St Ives plc

All rights reserved. No part of this book may be reproduced, transmitted
or stored in an information retrieval system in any form or by any means,
graphic, electronic or mechanical, including photocopying, taping and
recording, without prior written permission from the publisher.

British Library Cataloguing in Publication Data: a catalogue record
for this book is available from the British Library

ISBN 978-1-4063-1917-0

www.walker.co.uk

For lots of people...

Noah (welcome!)
Freya (welcome!)
Barbara
Nan
Jordan & Adelaide
Owen & Louise
Maia, Sasha & Thea
Thomas
Nell

Meet the residents...

Luke Watson

Cleo Farr

Resus Negative

Dixon

Sir Otto Sneer

Samuel Skipstone

Alston and Bella Negative

Eefa Everwell

Doug

Dr Skully

Niles Farr

Mr and Mrs Watson

Who lives where...

A Sheer Hall

B Central square

C Everwell's Emporium

D No. 2: The Crudlegs

E No. 5: The Movers

F No. 11: Twinkle

G No. 13: Luke Watson

H No. 14: Resus Negative

I No. 21: Eefa Everwell

J No. 22: Cleo Farr

K No. 26: The Headless Horseman

L No. 27: Femur Ribs

M No. 28: Doug, Turf and Berry

N No. 31: Kian Negative

O No. 32: Ryan Aire

P No. 39: The Skullys

Previously on Scream Street...

Mr and Mrs Watson were terrified when their son, Luke, first transformed into a werewolf. But that was nothing compared to their terror at being forcibly moved to Scream Street – and discovering there was no going back.

Determined to take his parents home, Luke enlisted the help of his new friends, Resus Negative, a wannabe vampire, and Cleo Farr, an Egyptian mummy, to find six relics left behind by the community's founding fathers. Only by collecting these magical artefacts would he be able to open a doorway back to his own world.

Just as Luke and his friends finally succeeded in their quest, Mr and Mrs Watson realized how happy Luke had become in his new home and decided to stay on in Scream Street. But the newly opened doorway was becoming a problem – Sir Otto Sneer, Scream Street's wicked landlord, was charging "normals" from Luke's world to visit what he called "the world's greatest freak show".

To protect Scream Street, Luke, Resus and Cleo must try to close the doorway by returning the relics to their original owners – and the next recipient is right on their doorstep…

Chapter One
The Lesson

The banshee threw back her head and wailed. Her voice rose and fell, rattling windows and shaking ornaments. A vase of flowers juddered across the sideboard and dropped to the floor with a smash.

"THANK YOU!" Dr Skully roared over the din. "YOU CAN SIT DOWN NOW!" Favel

Tap finally came to a stop and smiled at her new classmates as she sat down at her desk.

In the front row, Resus Negative cautiously removed his hands from his ears. "Blimey!" he exclaimed. "If that's how banshees tell you their name, remind me never to ask for her address!"

"Or be anywhere near when she stubs her toe," smiled Cleo Farr.

Luke Watson shifted impatiently in his seat. "This is ridiculous," he muttered under his breath.

"Tell me about it," agreed Resus. "I can't believe we're back in school either."

"That's enough chatter, you three," said Dr Skully. "May I remind you that class has started. Now, let us turn our attention to the world of flora and fauna. Please all open your textbooks at chapter twelve. I'm happy to announce that this morning an expert on the subject of seeds and bulbs will be paying us a visit..."

The door opened and a large, tattooed man dressed in a pink tutu and tiara squeezed into the room. "Wotcha, kids!" grunted Twinkle the fairy.

Dr Skully grinned – an eerie sight on a face without lips. "Twinkle has very kindly agreed to tell us everything he knows on the subject of beans."

"That's right," grunted the fairy, stomping around the class to place a single, brown bean in front of each pupil. "These are magic beans, and even though they're quite valuable, they should never be taken as full or part payment for a cow or any other farm animal. I once knew an old woman whose son set off to market wiv a cow..."

Kian Negative raised his hand, interrupting the story.

"Wot?" asked Twinkle.

"I'm a vampire!" he proclaimed.

Twinkle looked confused for a moment, then continued. "So, as I was sayin', I once knew an old woman whose son..."

Luke, squashed in next to Cleo at a desk designed for one, sighed heavily. "We shouldn't be here," he moaned.

"I know," said Resus. "Who wants to learn about this rubbish?"

"I don't mean that," retorted Luke. "I mean that we should be off returning the next relic! Zeal Chillchase promised that lessons would be cancelled until we'd given them all back."

"He can't help it if G.H.O.U.L. is starting to get suspicious," Cleo whispered. "He said things have to look as normal as possible – and there are so many kids living in Scream Street now, it'd look odd if they weren't all in school."

Luke had to admit she was right. When he had first been moved to Scream Street, Resus and Cleo had been the only other pupils taught by the skeletal Dr Skully. But now there were seven children crammed into the teacher's dining room. Sitting next to Resus was his young cousin, Kian – and behind them was the ghostly Ryan Aire and his brother, Finn, with Favel Tap perched at the end of their desk. Each of the new pupils was busy scribbling notes into his or her exercise book on the uses of magic beans.

Resus held his bean up to the light and squinted at it. "You're not telling me there's a whole plant in there, waiting to get out."

"It can't be any more eager to get out than I am," hissed Luke.

"Me too," said Cleo. "Eefa's sister is arriving from Australia this morning with her baby daughter. She said I can go over and play with her later."

14

Resus pulled a face. "What is it with girls and babies? You go all loopy at the mere sight of what is basically just a poo and puke machine!"

"I hope you three are taking in everything Twinkle is telling us," boomed Dr Skully's voice.

The trio looked up to see their teacher glaring at them from his desk.

"Yes, sir," fibbed Luke. "Cleo and I were just helping Resus to understand how plants might grow from these beans."

Dr Skully gave him a brief nod then turned back to Twinkle. "Please continue," he said.

"Then in the morning, both the boy and his mother were amazed to find their humble little cottage in the shadow of a massive…"

Luke waited until he was sure Dr Skully wasn't watching them before he continued in a whisper, "Every minute we sit listening to this, Sneer's charging more normals to come and poke around Scream Street. We have to get out of here!"

"You're right, but how?" said Cleo.

"Leave that to me," said Resus with a wink, then he began to root around in his cape.

A few moments later, Cleo raised her hand. "Sir!" she called out. "Dr Skully!"

The skeleton pulled his attention away from where Twinkle was drawing a golden harp on the blackboard. "Yes, Miss Farr?" he said. "What is it now?"

"I don't think Resus is feeling very well, sir!" The vampire was resting his head on the desk and moaning softly.

The new pupils watched as Dr Skully stood and made his way over to the trio. "If this is another of your jokes, Master Negative…"

"I don't think it is, sir," said Luke. "He said he wasn't feeling right this morning."

Dr Skully's fingers clicked as he rested his hands on his bony hips. "What's the matter, Resus?" he demanded.

A gasp went round the room as the vampire lifted his head to reveal a face covered with fat, glistening molluscs.

"I think I've got slug flu," he croaked.

"Slug flu?" said Luke with a smile as he, Resus and Cleo dodged between crowds of normals at the edge of the square.

Resus grinned back at him. "Yup! The only illness that's infectious to just about everyone in Scream Street. If Dr Skully hadn't cancelled class, he'd have had an epidemic on his hands!"

"But how do you know those slugs weren't really infected?" asked Cleo.

"Because they're not slugs — they're leeches," said Resus. "Dave had babies."

"Your pet leech had babies?" Cleo exclaimed. "But he's a boy, isn't he?"

Resus shrugged. "I don't think it matters with leeches. Besides, who cares? Those little fellas are adorable!"

"Look who's going gaga over babies now," laughed Cleo.

"But Dr Skully spent years in a science lab," said Luke. "Surely he can tell the difference between slugs and leeches."

"That was a risk," Resus admitted. "But I was willing to bet he wouldn't get close enough to see!"

As the trio arrived at 27 Scream Street, Luke made sure no one was watching, then he swung open the gate and they stepped through, following the path around to the back garden and stopping in front of a large marble tomb. Above the entrance were inscribed the words:

The final resting place of
Femur Ribs

Cleo sighed. "I come here sometimes just to sit and read," she said. "It's comforting to know that one of the founding fathers is just a few metres away."

"*Most* of one of the founding fathers," Resus corrected her, pulling Femur's skull out of his cloak and handing it to Luke.

"Goodness me!" exclaimed the skull. "That sun's a little bright."

"I'm sorry, Femur," said Luke, turning to shield it from the glare. "I forgot how dark it would be inside Resus's cape."

"Not a problem, young Luke," smiled Femur. "But what, may I ask, are we doing out here?"

18

"Sir Otto has filled Scream Street with normals," Cleo explained. "And we have to return all the relics in order to close the doorway and get rid of them."

Femur's skull eyed the entrance to her tomb. "You mean you're putting me back together?"

"If you don't mind…" said Resus.

"Of course not," she smiled. "I must admit it has felt a little unusual being separated from the rest of my body!"

"We'll have you back in one piece in no time," Luke assured her. He made his way over to the sealed entrance to the tomb. "Now… How do you open this thing?"

Chapter Two
The Tomb

Luke wedged the crowbar into the thin gap around the edge of the door and pulled as hard as he could. The tool strained against the effort, bending slightly as Luke leant into it with all of his weight. His palms began to sweat – causing the crowbar to slip from his grasp and

catapult away from him, spinning past Resus and embedding itself in the wall of the house with a loud *boi-oi-oi-oing!*

"Watch it!" cried the vampire, reaching up to check that his ear was still in place. "You nearly took my head off!"

"Sorry," said Luke. "I thought I had it moving then."

"And did you?"

Luke shook his head. "Not so much as a millimetre!"

"No luck here, either," called Cleo from above them. The boys looked up to see her peering down at them from the roof of the tomb. "I can't see any way in at all."

Luke sighed. The trio had been trying to find a way into the crypt for more than an hour now. The stone door was smooth and cold, with nothing that looked as though it could be used as a handle or lock. No amount of pushing, sliding or lifting would move it. Even worse, a small crowd of normals had begun to watch proceedings with interest over the garden hedge.

"I wonder if Doug's having better luck," said Cleo, using a length of bandage tied around the neck of a nearby gargoyle to climb down.

As she spoke, the ground at their feet began to rumble and a green fist punched up through the lawn, patting the grass around it until one of the twisted digits made contact with the leather of Resus's shoe. Satisfied that he was in the right place, Doug the zombie pushed up through the earth.

"Dude!" exclaimed the living corpse. "Am I glad to get out from under there!"

"Any way in from below?" Luke asked him.

Doug shook his head, dislodging a colony of beetles nestled in his greasy hair. "No way, man," he replied. "That baby's locked down tighter than a lead-lined blood vault! I broke three fingers just trying to find my way back up."

"This is ridiculous," groaned Resus. "There must be *some* way in."

Doug gazed up at the vampire. "Dude – I heard you got a dose of the slug flu!"

Cleo rolled her eyes. "That didn't take long to get out, did it?"

"I'm fine," Resus assured him. "The slug flu story was just an excuse to get out of class early."

Doug grinned through a mouthful of decaying

teeth. "Don't let the man pin you down, little vampire! Shame about the slugs, though. I was hoping to get one or two from you for an afternoon snack."

"There's Ryan!" said Luke, spotting a young ghost among the rapidly growing crowd. "Hey, Ryan – over here!"

The spectre shimmered away and then materialized again beside the group gathered by the tomb. "What are you guys trying to *do*?" he asked.

"The impossible, by the look of it," replied Resus.

Ryan peered at him. "I thought you had slug flu…"

"Don't you start!"

"We need to get inside this tomb," Luke explained, "but there doesn't seem to be any way to open the door. Would you mind giving us a hand?"

"Sure," said the ghost. "How?"

"You can float through walls, right?" said Luke. "Can you float through there and see if there's any sort of mechanism to open the door from the inside?"

"No problem," replied Ryan, and taking a

deep breath, he lifted his feet off the ground and sped towards the tomb. The watching tourists let out an impressed *Oooh!* as he sailed smoothly across the garden ... and smashed straight into the granite doorway.

"Ryan!" yelled Cleo, dashing over as the ghost crashed to the ground. Clear ectoplasm ran from his nose like blood. "Are you OK?"

"I… I think so," he answered. "I just couldn't get through. It's like there's some sort of force field around the whole thing."

"Could you materialize inside?" asked Resus.

"I don't think so," Ryan replied. "I get the feeling that whoever sealed this doesn't want anyone to get in."

"We'll see about that," grunted Resus, pulling a sledgehammer from his cape. "Let's try a more direct approach…"

"You can't break into the tomb of a founding father!" Cleo cried.

"Why not?" demanded the vampire, taking a couple of practice swings. "It'd be worth it to get rid of that lot." The crowd of nosy normals was now backed up along the street. Some of the smaller children sat on their parents' shoulders,

 24

while others tried to find footholds in the garden hedge to get themselves a better view.

Cleo turned to Femur for support, but the skull didn't seem worried. "Young Resus is right," she admitted. "If you want to get Scream Street back to how it should be, you might have to cause a little damage."

The vampire stuck his tongue out at the mummy. "There you go," he grinned. "Straight from the skeleton's mouth!"

Cleo lifted up her hands in surrender. "OK," she said. "Do what you want."

Resus cricked his neck from side to side, then, taking careful aim, he swung the sledgehammer round and hit the exact centre of the crypt door. The steel head of the hammer instantly shattered into dust.

"Ow!" yelled Resus, dropping the handle and rubbing at his wrists. "That's going to hurt in the morning!"

"With any luck," came a satisfied voice from behind them. The group turned to see a smug Sir Otto Sneer pushing his way through the crowd of normals.

"You've done something to the tomb, haven't

you?" Luke demanded angrily.

Scream Street's landlord bit down hard on his cigar. "I'm not Sneer," he hissed. "It's me, Zeal Chillchase."

Luke didn't look convinced. "Prove it!"

Sir Otto pulled his cigar from his mouth, and with a sound like running water his facial features rearranged themselves into those of the G.H.O.U.L. Tracker while the rest of him remained identical to Sir Otto.

"Now, *that's* a freaky look," Resus commented.

"Why are you disguised like that?" asked Luke.

"I'm trying to avoid the attention of G.H.O.U.L.," replied Zeal. He looked up at the ever-growing crowd on the other side of the hedge. "Something I see you've completely given up on!"

"It's not our fault," Luke protested. "We can't get inside Femur's crypt! Can you do anything?"

"Not with the crypt," said Chillchase. "But I might be able to help with the crowd…" He shapeshifted his face back to that of Scream Street's landlord and turned to address the normals. "Ladies and gentlemen!" he bellowed. "Follow me for an exclusive behind-the-scenes tour of the sewers. Rats aplenty, and maybe a guffing goblin or two thrown in for good measure!"

"OK," sighed Luke as the crowd dispersed, "what do we know about the tomb?"

"That it can't be opened," said Resus. "At least not by anything we've tried so far."

"There's no way in from below," said Doug.

"Or through the roof," added Cleo.

"And I can't float through the walls *or* materialize inside," Ryan finished.

Luke turned to him thoughtfully. "You said it felt like there was some sort of force field surrounding the tomb, didn't you."

The ghost nodded. "It was as if the whole thing was wrapped in glass."

The group stood silently for a moment, stumped. Then, with the flapping of delicate wings, Twinkle the fairy landed among them. "I couldn't help overhear," he sniffed. "But it's not glass – it's magic."

"Magic?" repeated Luke. "The tomb is sealed with magic?"

The fairy licked his finger and stretched out his tattooed arm towards the crypt. As his hand drew closer, a shower of pink sparks erupted in the air like a miniature fireworks display. "Powerful magic," he confirmed.

"Can you break the spell?" asked Resus. "Do you think you can get us inside?"

Twinkle considered for a moment, then his brow furrowed. "You told Dr Skully you had slug flu…"

Resus swallowed a frustrated scream. "I haven't got slug flu, OK?" he snapped. "It was just a way to get out of that boring lesson – no offence."

"None taken," grunted the fairy. "I was minutes away from fakin' an allergy to chalk myself!"

"So?" prompted Cleo. "Can you get past the spell around Femur's tomb?"

Twinkle shook his head. "I can't do nuffink about magic that strong," he said apologetically. "But I know someone who can…"

Chapter Three
The Baby

"Peek-a-boo!" Cleo pulled her hands away from her eyes and grinned at the child in front of her. The toddler giggled joyfully.

Resus looked on from his vantage point behind the counter in Everwell's Emporium. "I *knew* she'd go gaga for that thing as soon as we got here."

"That *thing* is my niece, Poppy," Eefa Everwell pointed out. "And if you want my help, I suggest you start being a little kinder about her!"

The vampire blushed beneath his white face paint, which gave his cheeks a strange pink glow. "Sorry," he muttered. "I didn't mean she was… She's a lovely little, er … niece. She must be, what? Six years old? Seven?"

"She's nearly two," Eefa corrected. "And my sister has made a flying visit to introduce her to me – so I suggest we get on with whatever it is you're after."

"Fair enough," said Resus, glad to change the subject. "Luke?"

But Luke didn't reply. With his chin resting on his hands, he was staring in adoration at Eefa's sister, Luella. The young witch's long blonde hair shimmered in the light as she joined in her daughter's game, and her pale blue eyes seemed to sparkle like the clear water of a tropical—

"LUKE!"

The cry jerked Luke back to reality. "Yes?" he grunted, wiping drool from the corner of his mouth. "What?"

"Eefa wants to know how you'd like her to help us," continued the vampire. "But you were lost somewhere in her sister's enchantment charm!"

"I was not," retorted Luke. "I was just thinking how, er … how alike she and her daughter look."

"Thank you," smiled Luella. "Whoever knew that Scream Street would be home to such a charming young gentleman?"

"Oh, I … er…" Luke's mouth opened and closed like a goldfish. "You really didn't… That is…"

Eefa stepped in for him. "Luella is beautiful – with or without her enchantment charm," she said. "And yes, Poppy takes after her mum. But that's not what you came to talk to me about, is it?"

Luke finally tore his gaze away from the visiting witch. "No, it's not," he confirmed. "We need to return the fifth founding father's relic – Femur Ribs's skull – but we can't get inside her tomb."

"Twinkle says it's been sealed by magic," added Resus.

The fairy looked up from a display case of ruby and sapphire tiaras. "S'right," he said. "Serious stuff it is, too. Not seen anyfink like it around here before."

"Will you please help us break through the spell?" Luke asked.

"Today?" said Eefa. "But I want to spend time with my sister. I only let you in because Cleo asked to see the baby."

"Could you just take a look at it?" begged Luke. "Please…"

"You could take your sister with you," suggested Resus. "You know the old saying – two witches are better than one."

Eefa's brow furrowed. "That's not a saying."

"Well, then – it should be," Resus persisted. "I'll bet there's no spell in Scream Street the Everwell sisters can't break through."

"Flattery will get you nowhere, Resus Negative," smiled the witch. "But even if Luella and I do go to examine this spell, what are we supposed to do with Poppy?"

"We'll look after her!" Resus said quickly. "I've been looking forward to spending time with her all morning."

Eefa looked surprised. "You have?"

"Of course," continued the vampire. "In fact, I clearly remember saying to Luke in class this morning that I couldn't wait for lessons to finish so I could come over here and play peek-a-boo with Polly."

"You mean *Poppy*," put in Luke with a barely disguised grin.

"Exactly!"

Eefa didn't look convinced. "I don't know…"

"She'll be fine with us," Resus urged. "Just look how good I am with children…"

Jumping down from his stool he hurried across the shop and put his cape over his face. Poppy's eyes widened in surprise.

"Now, watch the master entertainer at work…" With a flourish, Resus pulled the cape away and smiled his biggest, cheesiest smile. "Peek-a-boo!"

The effect was instant. Poppy took one look at the vampire, buried her face in Cleo's shoulder and screamed.

"What's wrong?" asked Resus, moving behind the mummy so he could see Poppy's face. "You were OK when Cleo did it!"

Catching sight of him again, Poppy began to sob uncontrollably and tried to climb over Cleo's shoulder to get away.

"Poppy!" cried Luella, reaching out to take her daughter. But the toddler was in hysterics and beginning to act very strangely indeed. Her eyes flashed red and she bit down hard on her mother's outstretched hand.

"Ow!"

Suddenly there was a tearing sound and a long, sharp tail ripped through the back of Poppy's nappy, making a hole in her dress. Cleo screamed and dropped her to the floor, where she began gnashing and snarling.

"What's happening to her?" Luella wailed.

Poppy flicked out a forked tongue and let loose a piercing screech. Pushing past Cleo, she scampered over to some shelves and began to climb up them like a monkey. Once she reached the top, she began to pull out clumps of her own hair and hiss angrily.

Eefa put her arm around her terrified sister.

"What's going on?" sobbed Luella. "What's happened to my baby?"

"That's not your baby," said Twinkle, staring

35

up at the child. Her scalp was now red raw and beginning to bleed. "I fink it's a changeling!"

"A what?" demanded Luke.

"Let me see!" cried a voice that came from the direction of Luke's jeans pocket. Luke pulled out a golden book with *The G.H.O.U.L. Guide* embossed along the spine and turned it so that the face on the cover could look at the creature.

"Oh dear," said Samuel Skipstone. "I'm sorry to say that Twinkle is correct. That is indeed a changeling."

Luke continued to watch the baby, whose tail was now swishing back and forth angrily. "What's one of those?"

The book opened and began to flick through its pages until it found the correct entry. There was an article accompanied by an illustration of a beast not very different from the one they were all looking at.

"Changelings are a kind of shapeshifter," explained the author. "They were once used by dark fairies – the original occupants of the fairy realm. They roamed the land stealing children and leaving replicas in their places."

"But there hasn't been no dark fairies for years and years," said Twinkle.

"Not until now," agreed Skipstone. The author of *The G.H.O.U.L. Guide* had spent his life researching Scream Street and similar communities before committing his spirit to the pages of his work. There was very little he didn't know about G.H.O.U.L.'s unusual residents.

"So … that isn't really Poppy?" asked Eefa.

"I'm afraid not," replied Skipstone. "It's a copy, left behind by whoever took the real Poppy."

"It's not a very good copy, if you ask me," said Resus. "I might not know much about babies – but the tail and forked tongue are a bit of a giveaway."

"Something must have scared it to cause such a reaction," said Skipstone. "Some changelings have been known to remain undetected for many years."

"So, where's my baby?" asked Luella tearfully. "Who's taken her, and why?"

"That I cannot say," replied the author. "And neither can the changeling. They know nothing of their true purpose, and can only carry out the most basic imitation of the child they have replaced. Sadly, that deception is more than enough to fool many families – unless they discover their changeling's secret, of course."

"Secret?" repeated Cleo. "What do you mean?"

"Every changeling conceals a secret; a hidden ability or behaviour that makes them unique," explained Skipstone. "When the creatures were in common use, it was often the only way to tell them apart."

"What sort of ability?" asked Resus.

The G.H.O.U.L. Guide flipped over a page to reveal a long list. "Some of them could fly or become invisible, others could detect gold or speak a hundred languages. This list contains only the secrets harboured by changelings I was personally able to research."

Cleo eyed the hissing child as Luke closed the book and slipped it back into his pocket. "So, this little thing has a secret…"

"Let's hope it's the language one," said Resus. "Then it might be able to tell us where and when it was swapped for the real Poppy."

Luella dissolved into another flood of tears and Eefa did her best to comfort her. "Where's my little girl?" she wailed.

Luke glanced at Resus and Cleo before answering. "We don't know," he admitted. "But we're going to find her."

Chapter Four
The Plan

Resus pulled Luke aside. "We're going to find Poppy?" he whispered. "How?"

Luke shrugged. "I don't know," he said. "But we have to try." He paused for a moment. "I remember when my mum had her first werewolf transformation. I thought I'd lost her; that there

was some sort of monster in her place – I can imagine how Eefa's sister must be feeling."

"It's a nice idea," said Resus. "But why us?"

"We can't expect Luella to go looking for her, the state she's in," said Luke, watching Eefa pour her sister a cup of tea. "And apart from her, we're the only ones who've ever really been outside Scream Street."

"He's right," agreed Cleo. "We are the most qualified to do this."

"Maybe so," said Resus, "but don't we already have enough on our plates? Aren't we supposed to be finding a way into Femur's crypt?"

Eefa handed the tea to her trembling sister and then came over to join the trio. "If you do this for us," she said, taking Luke's hand, "Luella and I will help all we can. If you manage to find Poppy, we'll break that shield spell and get you into the tomb."

Luke smiled. "You've got yourself a deal."

"But whoever's got Poppy could have taken her anywhere in the world," Resus pointed out. "We can't just start walking and hope we eventually bump into her!"

"He's got a point," Cleo admitted.

 42

Luke turned to look at the changeling. The creature had relaxed a little and was busy stuffing its mouth with sweets from a glass jar on a nearby shelf. "There's got to be some sort of clue to get us started."

"Well, it's an ugly little critter," said Resus. "Is that a clue?"

"Don't be so cruel," Cleo snapped.

"I'm just saying I don't think I'll be going in for another game of peek-a-boo!"

"Just as well," said Cleo. "You were the one to frighten it."

Luke's eyes widened. "He was, wasn't he! The changeling took one look at Resus and then flipped out."

Resus bristled. "You're no oil painting yourself, Watson."

"I don't mean that," said Luke impatiently. "But the baby was quite happily playing with Cleo until you tried to join in." He took a step away and looked from Cleo to Resus and back again. "What's the difference between the two of you?"

"How long have you got?" Cleo asked.

"It'll be the face," Luke said, ignoring her. "When you play peek-a-boo, all you see is the

other person's face. But why would that make a difference?"

Cleo shrugged. "I'm pretty much covered in bandages, so the changeling won't have seen much of my face to begin with. It's just the eyes and the smile, really."

"Hm," said Luke. He turned to Resus. "Try to play with her again."

"Are you daft?" exclaimed the vampire. "Have you seen the teeth on that thing?"

"I'm hoping she's more interested in yours. Now, do it!"

With a sigh, Resus hid his face behind his cape and went to stand by the shelves. Whipping the cape away, he grinned up at the changeling and shouted, "Peek-a-boo!" The changeling screeched in terror and leapt across to another shelf, then began to hurl model unicorns at the children below.

"OK," said Luke. "Try again, but this time take your fangs out first…"

Resus unclipped his false fangs and stuffed them into his pocket. He steeled himself for another scream as he pulled the cape away a second time. "Peek-a-boo!"

44

To his amazement, the changeling collapsed into a fit of giggles. Its tail began to shrink and curly golden locks appeared through it's scalp, covering the bald patches.

"It's the fangs," breathed Cleo. "The changeling's scared of vampires!"

Resus pulled his teeth back out of his pocket and stared at them. He'd never had that effect on anyone before, and secretly he felt a little proud.

"Skipstone said that dark fairies used to swap changelings for children," said Luke. "Could there be a link between dark fairies and vampires?" He turned to Twinkle. "I don't suppose there are any vampires in the fairy realm, are there?"

Twinkle's bottom lip began to quiver, then he suddenly burst into tears. "Just one!" he bawled, running from the shop and out into the square.

"Well, I wasn't expecting that," admitted Resus. "We should go and find him." He made for the door, but Cleo stopped him.

"Aren't you forgetting something?" she asked.

Resus shrugged. "I don't think so."

Cleo gestured to the changeling, who now looked exactly like Poppy once again. "We have to take her with us, dummy."

"We can't take that thing with us!" cried Resus.

"We don't have any choice," said Luke. "She's our only hope of finding out where the switch took place."

"All right," sighed Resus, "have it your way. But if it starts biting and scratching again, don't say I didn't warn you."

"How will we get her down?" asked Cleo.

"Don't look at me," snorted Resus. "You're the one with all the bright ideas!"

The changeling let out a loud burp and then giggled.

"Maybe she's hungry," suggested Cleo. She

pulled a tiny, brown object from her bandages and held it up towards the little girl. "Here you go…"

"What's that?" asked Luke.

"The magic bean Twinkle gave us in class this morning."

"The changeling has been taught to mimic a little girl, not a hamster," scoffed Luke. "What's Poppy's favourite food?" he asked Luella.

"What does it matter?" the witch sniffed. "That's not really her!"

"No, it's not," he said, "but the changeling has learned to act exactly like Poppy – so if we give her something Poppy likes, it might just work."

"Well, she does love apples," said Luella.

"Coming right up," announced Resus, pulling a large, red apple from his cape and tossing it to Cleo. As soon as the changeling saw it, she jumped down from the shelf and into the mummy's arms.

Luella reached out and stroked the changeling gently on the cheek. "She looks so like her," she croaked, her tears beginning to flow again.

"We'll be back with the real Poppy before you know it," Luke assured her. And with a final

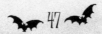

smile to Luella, he ushered Resus and Cleo out of the emporium, the changeling snuggled happily in the mummy's arms.

They found Twinkle sitting on the kerb outside, dabbing his eyes with a frilly handkerchief. "Do you fink they noticed?" he asked.

"What, that you burst into tears and ran off like a big girl's blouse," said Resus. "Nope. No one noticed at all."

"That's good," sniffed the fairy. "I didn't want to give Eefa's sister another fing to worry about."

"I think she's about as worried as she's going to get," said Cleo.

Twinkle fought back his own tears. "But… But she knows you're taking that fing into the fairy realm to try to find the real little girl…"

Luke nodded. "Is that going to be a problem?"

"Y-yes!" A bubble of pink, sparkly snot burst from Twinkle's nose as he began to cry again. "The fairy realm is at war!"

Chapter Five
The Attack

Luke, Resus and Cleo peered through the Hex Hatch into an idyllic woodland scene. Beams of sunlight dappled through the trees and skipped playfully across a small clearing. Birds trilled happy melodies and a family of deer pranced across a path of red brick that wound lazily away into the distance.

"Well," said Resus eventually. "It doesn't exactly look like a warzone."

"And I never imagined a Hex Hatch could look like this!" said Cleo, examining the window in the air. Pink sparkles fizzed around the edges of the newly opened entrance to the fairy realm. "It's an overdose of cute."

Twinkle had opened the Hex Hatch in a secluded spot at the rear of Everwell's Emporium, but when Luke asked him which part of the realm it linked to, the fairy had resumed his sobbing and flown off.

"What do you reckon?" asked Luke as he watched a pair of butterflies dance across the glade. "Is it safe to go in?"

As if in answer, the changeling jumped out of Cleo's arms and through the Hex Hatch into the woodland glade, where she began to toddle about and collect flowers.

"Ditto seems to think it's OK," said Cleo.

Resus frowned. "Ditto?"

Cleo nodded. "Well, she's not the real Poppy – so we can't keep calling her that. I thought I'd come up with a new name."

"Fair enough, but *Ditto*?"

"I think it suits her," said Cleo. "It means 'a copy of something'," she added helpfully.

"I know what it means," scoffed Resus. "I'm not as dumb as you seem to think I look!" Then his brow furrowed as he tried to work out if he'd just insulted himself.

Cleo rolled her eyes and climbed through the Hex Hatch after the changeling, hurrying to catch up with her before she ventured too far.

Luke and Resus followed, and together they set off along the red brick path.

Half an hour later, they came to a bridge that crossed a clear, trickling stream. They decided to take a rest and sat watching Ditto collect up pebbles and toss them into the sparkling water.

"It's lovely here," sighed Cleo.

"I've been to worse places," agreed Resus. "Mainly since I've known you," he added, grinning at Luke.

Luke laughed and pulled *The G.H.O.U.L. Guide* from his pocket. "It's certainly hard to imagine anything bad ever happening here," he said. "I wonder what Twinkle was so worked up about? It's nice and quiet."

"A little *too* quiet, if you ask me," said Samuel Skipstone from the cover of the book. "I've only

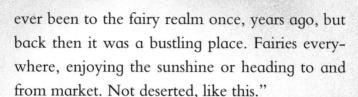

ever been to the fairy realm once, years ago, but back then it was a bustling place. Fairies everywhere, enjoying the sunshine or heading to and from market. Not deserted, like this."

"Maybe it's a public holiday?" suggested Resus.

Luke shrugged. "Or maybe Twinkle was right, and everyone's hidden themselves away because the fairy realm is at war."

Cleo heard a sound and turned to look down the road. "Nonsense," she said. "Look, there's someone coming now…"

Luke and Resus squinted against the bright sunlight to see a carriage heading their way. It was round and orange and pulled by two squat, brown horses.

"Is that… Is that a pumpkin?" asked Resus incredulously.

"Only if those horses have whiskers and large, pointy teeth," replied Luke.

"They're rats!" exclaimed Cleo as the coach drew nearer. "Who rides around in a pumpkin coach pulled by giant rats?"

By way of an answer, a face appeared, leering out of the window of the coach. At first it

appeared to be a skeleton, but as it drew closer the trio could see scraps of skin hanging off the emaciated frame. The figure was dressed in what appeared to be a dirty, torn ballgown, and clumps of straggly, dry hair whipped about her head in the breeze.

"I don't like the look of her," cried Resus.

"She seems to like us, though," said Luke. "She's coming straight for us!" He was right, the huge rats were thundering directly towards them, their dull fur spattered with dirt and dried blood and spittle foaming at their mouths.

"Quick – down here!" called Cleo, grabbing Ditto and sliding down the bank to take shelter under the bridge. Luke quickly dived after her. As Resus made to follow, he noticed that the strange creature in the pumpkin coach was gripping something in her withered hand – some kind of sparkling shoe.

"Why is she…?" he began.

With unexpected strength and accuracy, the woman hurled the shoe directly at Resus's head, catching him in the face with the sharp heel. Within seconds, blood was pouring from a gash just above his left eye.

Luke's hand appeared from under the bridge, grabbed Resus by the ankle and pulled him to safety.

Cleo took one look at the vampire and gasped. "What happened?" she hissed, tearing off a piece of bandage and using it to mop up the blood.

"That crazy woman threw a shoe at me!" Resus cried.

"A *shoe*?" exclaimed Luke.

Resus reached up and touched the gash. "Not just that – a glass shoe!"

The coach now thundered above them, shaking the bridge violently as it clattered over

the bricks. The woman in the back was cackling insanely and muttering to herself, "Bong! Bong! Hee hee hee! Must be home by midnight, deary!"

Luke peered out from their hiding place and was horrified to see the coach turning around. The scrawny woman had another slipper clutched in her putrid hand.

"She's coming back!" Luke cried. "We have to get out of here."

"We can't go up there," said Cleo. "We'll be sitting ducks."

"We could run for the trees," suggested Resus, blinking away the blood that was dripping down into his eye.

"Maybe *we* could make it," said Cleo, "but Ditto is far too slow – and I won't be able to run if I'm carrying her."

Resus opened his mouth to speak, but Cleo cut him off. "And before you say anything, no, we're not leaving her behind!"

"Maybe her secret is that she can fight off terrifying zombies with just her bare hands," suggested Resus.

"I don't think so," said Cleo as she hugged the trembling child.

"Then we're trapped," said Luke. "Shield your faces in case she throws the other shoe!" The group ducked – but instead of the coach, a vast white horse leapt over them, landing on the bridge in a shower of sparks as its hooves made contact with the stone.

On the back of the horse sat a handsome,

bronzed man with piercing blue eyes. He was dressed like a cowboy from a movie, and weapons of all descriptions were strapped to both his belt and the horse's saddle.

Resus stared up at him. "This is now officially weird…" he breathed.

The newcomer glanced at the vampire and sneered. "Stay down!" he growled.

Infuriated at the sight of the rider, the woman in the coach screeched and hurled her glass slipper straight at him.

Unfazed, the man waited until the shoe had almost reached him before snatching a sword from his side and slicing it right down the middle. The two glass halves flew over the side of the bridge and splashed harmlessly into the stream.

The gaunt woman let out a piercing scream and urged her carriage onwards. She was now almost upon the rider and his horse, who stood motionless on the bridge.

Fast as lightning, the rider sheathed his sword and produced a crossbow loaded with what appeared to be a thick, sharp arrow. He fired it at one of the two rats, spearing it in the leg. The creature let out a bellow of pain and turned, dragging the stinking chariot off the road and into the trees despite the anguished cries of its mistress. Before long, silence fell over the woodland again.

The man slotted another sharp stick into his crossbow and clipped it back onto his belt. "You can come out now," he grunted. "Skinderella has gone."

Luke was the first to climb up the bank. *"Skinderella?"* he said.

The rider nodded, the corners of his mouth curling into what might have been a smile as Resus, Cleo and Ditto joined their friend. "But we can't stay here. She'll be back once she's got control of the rats." He snapped the reins on his horse and it turned to continue its journey along the red brick path. "You're welcome, by the way."

Luke, Resus and Cleo hurried after their mysterious rescuer, Ditto clinging tightly to Cleo's hand. "Th-thank you," stammered Resus.

"Who are you?" demanded Cleo.

The rider took a wide-brimmed leather hat from his saddlebag and pressed it onto his head. "I'm Prince Harming," he drawled. "Vampire hunter."

Chapter Six
The Queen

Resus slid his hand into his pocket and ran a finger over his false fangs. "Did you say *vampire hunter?*" he asked, glancing nervously at his friends.

"Sure did," growled Prince Harming. "And there's only one vampire around here…" He whipped out a battered old hand mirror, which he held up in front of Resus's face. For a moment, the vampire thought the newcomer was trying to prove that he had no reflection. But suddenly the glass began to blur and ripple.

"It's changing!" said Cleo.

An indistinct image began to appear: a tall woman with long, dark hair, wearing a bright red dress and relaxing on a luxurious throne. The trio watched as she reached into a basket at her side and produced two cakes, handing one to a tiny, blonde-haired figure kneeling beside her.

"Who's that?" asked Luke.

Before Prince Harming could reply, the woman suddenly looked up, as though she could see the figures on the other side of the glass. She jumped up and ran across the throne room towards them. Luke, Resus and Cleo stepped back as the woman pointed at them with a red finger-nail and opened her mouth in a wicked sneer, revealing long, glistening fangs. Ditto screeched and ducked behind Cleo, a tail bursting through the back of her dress.

Prince Harming quickly slipped the mirror back into his pocket. Cleo spun round to comfort Ditto, who was beginning to tear out her hair again. Luke and Resus tried to catch their breath.

"That," said the hunter, "is the Crimson

Queen. The cause of everything that's wrong in the fairy realm."

"It felt like she could see us!" exclaimed Luke.

"She could," said Harming. "She might not be able to see her own reflection, being a vampire and all, but she sees anyone and everyone who ever looks into a mirror in this here land."

"That's impossible," scoffed Resus.

"I used to think that too," replied Prince Harming. "But it turns out she's got a magic mirror. It's where she keeps the fairies trapped."

Luke frowned. "She's trapped some fairies?"

"Not *some* fairies, boy – all of them. Every single one."

"And she keeps them in a mirror?" asked Resus. "Must be crowded in there."

"Don't reckon I know the specifics," said Prince Harming, "but I do know the Crimson Queen is as cruel as she is beautiful. Now the fairy folk are her prisoners, she can take whatever she wants from them. She lives a life of luxury while their old kingdom is overrun by creatures of terror."

"You mean like that zombie?" Luke said. "What did you call her? Skinderella?"

"Her and plenty more besides," replied the vampire hunter. "This is dangerous territory for a bunch of kids to be wanderin' around on their own. Who are you, anyway?"

"I'm Luke, and this is Resus and Cleo," said Luke. "We're, er ... tourists."

"Tourists?"

Resus nodded enthusiastically. "You know, seeing the sights, taking in the culture…"

"Uh-huh," grunted Prince Harming, although he didn't look convinced. He turned his horse round to face Cleo. "How's the babe doin'?"

Cleo was clutching Ditto tightly to her chest. "Seeing that woman scared the life out of her," the mummy replied. "Just like Resus did. Which confirms what we thought."

Luke and Resus gestured frantically for Cleo to keep quiet, but it was too late.

"And what's that?" demanded Prince Harming, twisting round in his saddle to look at the young vampire. "Might it have something to do with why you're dressed in a vampire cloak?" As he spoke, he unclipped his crossbow from his belt and began to thumb the sharp wooden stake loaded into it.

"What, *this*?" said Resus with a nervous smile. "This is just a costume. I'm not a vampire at all – look." He opened his mouth to display his lack of fangs.

"Then why would this here little 'un be scared of a slip of a boy like you?"

"It must be because Resus usually dresses in bright red – like the queen," Luke said quickly.

"Does he?" asked Cleo.

"Yes, he does," Luke insisted, trying to catch Cleo's eye. "Don't you remember, he had his red suit on this morning at school, but he had to get changed because the kid next to him had slug flu?"

"Oh, yeah," said Cleo, finally catching on. "And it's better to be safe than sorry, so we burnt his suit and now he's using this vampire costume we found in the dressing-up box!"

Prince Harming frowned. "You burnt his suit?"

Cleo flashed him her brightest smile. "You can't be too careful with slug flu!"

Thankfully, the vampire hunter was suddenly distracted by the sound of a scream echoing among the trees. He clipped his crossbow back

 64

onto his belt. "We'd better make tracks," he said. "And I think you youngsters ought to stick with me for the time being."

"Where are you heading?" asked Luke.

Prince Harming's lip curled into a snarl. "To the palace of the Crimson Queen," he said. "I got me some unfinished business there."

Luke nodded. "Then yes, we should stay with you."

Harming held out a hand to Cleo and Ditto. "Care to join me, ladies? If you promise not to set my clothes on fire, that is?"

Cleo blushed beneath her bandages as the tall, strong vampire hunter took her arm and lifted her and Ditto effortlessly onto the saddle in front of him.

"I'm afraid you two fellas are going to have to do a little walking…"

"That's OK," smiled Luke. Resus said nothing, his eyes still fixed on the vampire hunter's loaded crossbow.

And with that, Prince Harming clicked his heels and rode on, leading the children towards the palace of the Crimson Queen.

The group walked in silence for about an hour. The only sounds were the horse's hooves clopping steadily along the path, and the occasional desperate shriek from somewhere deep in the woods – but these seemed to be getting more distant as time went on.

Ditto had now recovered from her fright and she sat contentedly in Cleo's lap, her newly restored curls bobbing to the rhythmic steps of Prince Harming's steed.

"What is it you can do?" Cleo asked her, wishing she could discover the changeling's hidden secret. "Can you fly?" She lifted the toddler up and spread her arms in case it would encourage her to become airborne, but the baby squealed

with fright and reached out for the mummy with shaking hands.

"OK, then it's not that," said Cleo, cuddling Ditto to her chest. "I guess you get to keep your secret a little while longer."

Luke marched along behind the horse, keeping a sharp look-out, staring hard into the shadows among the trees on either side of the path.

Resus, however, was starting to struggle. "My head's really hurting," he admitted eventually, slumping against the trunk of a large oak tree.

Prince Harming pulled on his reins and dismounted to examine the vampire's wound. "Looks like there might be a sliver of glass in there," he said. "You'd do best to clean that out before it gets infected."

 67

Resus took a first-aid kit and a small mirror out of his cloak. He had just lifted the mirror up to check the cut when the vampire hunter knocked it out of his hand. The glass shattered as the mirror hit the ground.

"Are you crazy, boy?" he demanded, grinding what was left of the mirror to dust beneath his boot. "Why don't you just invite the Crimson Queen over for dinner?"

"I… I'm sorry," Resus muttered. "I guess I wasn't thinking."

"Too right you weren't thinking," growled Harming. "Now, get down to the water and clean that cut before it lets any more madness inside that head of yours!"

Sheepishly, Resus scuttled down the shallow bank to kneel beside the stream that still wound its way beside the path.

It seemed like a good time for them all to take a break, and Luke reached up to help Cleo and Ditto down from the horse. "That was a bit harsh, wasn't it?" whispered the mummy.

"I thought so too," hissed Luke. "But I suppose he's right: we can't risk being caught by this Crimson Queen."

Cleo glanced round to check the vampire hunter was out of earshot, and she saw he was busy chopping down a nearby branch with his sword. "Luke," she said quietly, "I saw something in the mirror, just before the queen came running at us. She had a little girl with her. I think it might have been Poppy."

Luke nodded. "I saw her too. I've been waiting for a chance to talk to you and Resus about it."

"It was the Crimson Queen who took Poppy and left the changeling behind, wasn't it?"

"It looks that way."

Cleo breathed a sigh of relief. "At least we know she's safe."

"Safe until Prince Vampire Hunter charges in, all crossbows blazing," Luke pointed out.

"Do you think we should tell him why we're here?" asked Cleo.

Luke shook his head. "Not for the moment," he said. "We don't know how—"

"I reckon we should rest here for a while," announced Prince Harming, striding over. The pair hurriedly stopped their whispered conversation and smiled in agreement, trying not to look guilty.

The vampire hunter snapped his newly acquired branch in two and began to sharpen the end of one of the sticks. "Best tell your friend our plans," he said.

"Resus!" Luke called down to the figure kneeling at the edge of the stream. "No need to rush, we're staying here for a while."

But Resus wasn't listening. He was staring into the face of the Crimson Queen.

Chapter Seven
The Offer

Resus was dabbing at the gash on his fore-head with a handkerchief he had soaked in the stream, when suddenly his reflection rippled and changed into that of the Crimson Queen.

"Boo!" she said.

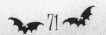

Resus jumped and tumbled forwards, putting his hands out to stop himself from falling in. He glanced over his shoulder to see if the others were close.

"Don't call them, Resus," said the queen gently.

Resus turned back to stare at her. "How do you know my name?"

The queen smiled. "Oh, I know more about you than you could possibly imagine. I can see your every thought and desire. For instance, I know what you really are…"

Resus could feel his false fangs in his pocket. They seemed to burn red hot against his leg. "You're bluffing."

"Am I?" asked the queen, amused. "Then why don't we call Prince Harming over for a bit of a chat?" She licked her fangs with the tip of her tongue. "How do you like your *stakes*, by the way? Rare? Medium? Well done?"

Resus swallowed hard. "What do you want from me?"

"It's more a case of what you want from me, my dear," the Crimson Queen said. "There's this little thing, for a start." Reaching down, she lifted the small blonde child into view and gave her a kiss on the cheek.

"Poppy!" Resus exclaimed. The toddler giggled at the sound of her name. "What have you done with her?"

"Why, nothing," said the queen. "I don't even want her, if you must know the truth. You can come and take her back any time you want."

"But, the changeling…"

"…was nothing to do with me," the queen said firmly, putting Poppy back down. "I just woke up one day and this little treasure was here."

Resus's brow furrowed. "You didn't take her and leave Ditto in her place?"

The queen laughed, but it wasn't an altogether pleasant sound. "What would I want with a child?" she asked innocently. "And somebody else's, at that? If I were ever lonely, I'd use magic to create a companion."

"Magic?"

The Crimson Queen casually examined her immaculate fingernails. "More powerful than you could ever imagine, Resus." She smiled widely. "But why *tell* you, when I could *show* you? Wash your cut in the stream."

"Why?" asked Resus, nervously. "What are you going to do?"

"Help you, dear boy – now, do it!"

Obediently, Resus scooped a handful of clear water from the stream and splashed it onto his forehead. The cut tingled for a second, then stopped hurting altogether. "The pain," he gasped. "It's gone!"

"So has the wound itself," declared the queen. She clicked her fingers and her image shimmered away to be replaced once more by Resus's reflection. He was amazed to see that the cut had completely disappeared.

"That's incredible!" he laughed.

The Crimson Queen's face came floating back again. "Isn't it just?" she said excitedly, then her expression became more serious. "Now, imagine what my powers could do for Scream Street."

Resus was thrown for a moment. "Scream Street?" he said uncertainly.

The queen sighed. "All that running around, returning relics... Sounds like a lot of hard work to me."

"How do you know about—"

"Why, I could get rid of the normals and close

that pesky doorway with a single click of my fingers!"

"That would be brilliant," breathed Resus. "Everything would just—" He stopped suddenly. "Wait a minute… Why should I trust you? Prince Harming said you'd trapped all the fairies in your magic mirror."

The queen's face fell, as though Resus's words had hurt her. "And you believe a man whose sole purpose in life is to find and kill vampires like you and me?"

Resus felt his cheeks flush. "I… I don't know…"

The Crimson Queen held out her hand. "Join me, Resus," she said softly. "We could do so much good together. You could be the saviour of Scream Street. Why let Luke take all the glory? We know who's really doing all the work."

Resus's head was spinning. "I have to … have to t-talk to my friends," he stammered.

"No, you don't," the queen insisted. "They won't believe a word you say. You can be so much more than this, Resus. You can be … a real vampire!"

The words echoed around Resus's mind. "A

real vampire?" he croaked. "Like my mum and dad?"

"Exactly like them, Resus," the queen smiled, her hand reaching closer and closer. "Join me and you will finally become a worthy descendant in the glorious bloodline of Count Negatov!"

Resus's heart pounded as he stretched his own arm out towards the water. "After all these years, I'd finally be…"

"There you are!" cried Luke, bounding down the bank. "We were beginning to think you'd fallen in."

Resus shook his head. "N-no," he said, trying to steady his voice. "I was just—" He looked back at the water to see his own reflection staring back up at him. The Crimson Queen had gone.

Luke sat down beside his friend. "Hey," he exclaimed. "Your head's better!"

Resus touched the spot where the gash had been. "Yeah," he said. "It looked worse than it was. Once I'd washed the blood away, there was nothing to see."

"That's a relief." Luke checked they were alone, then lowered his voice. "Cleo and I thought we saw Poppy in the Crimson Queen's throne room," he said. "Although we only got a quick glance so we might have been wrong."

"No, she's there," Resus confirmed. "I, er … I mean, I'm sure I saw her as well."

"Good," said Luke. "If we go with Prince Harming to the Crimson Queen's castle, we might be able to get Poppy out before he starts firing his wooden stakes everywhere."

"I don't like him," muttered Resus. "Or what he's planning to do."

"He's trying to free all the fairies she has trapped in that mirror of hers," said Luke.

"We've only got Harming's word for it that that's what she's done," Resus snapped. "How do you know we can trust him?"

Luke was taken aback. "Well, he did save us from that weirdo, Skinderella…"

Resus began to lose his temper. "For all we know, he was the one who set her on us in the first place!"

"Why would he do that?"

Resus shrugged. "I dunno," he said. "Maybe to ride in and get all the glory when he saved us? He does seem to think he's some kind of hero cowboy, after all."

"That's ridiculous."

"Is it?" said Resus. "He seemed to know an awful lot about the queen."

"That's his job," Luke retorted.

"No," barked Resus. "His job is to kill vampires! Vampires like me, like my mum and dad…"

They froze as a child's scream pierced the calm of the woods.

"Ditto!" cried Luke.

The boys raced up the bank to find the clearing completely engulfed in a mini tornado. Leaves spun through the air, along with Prince Harming's assortment of weapons. Cleo clung onto a tree with one hand, her other holding tightly to Ditto, desperately trying to stop the changeling from being dragged into the whirlwind.

Luke dashed towards them but stopped as a twisted animal-like face appeared in the midst of the ferocious gale. It sneered at him briefly then was lost among the debris. Two others appeared soon after, both laughing with delight at the chaos around them.

"What are those things?" yelled Resus.

"They're poltergeists!" shouted Prince Harming

from across the clearing. "And they're being controlled by *her*!"

Luke and Resus followed the vampire hunter's gaze to see the ghost of a young girl standing serenely in the centre of the tornado. Brushing a few stray leaves from her dress, she flung her hands into the air and began to wave them around as though conducting an orchestra.

"Who is *that*?" bellowed Luke.

"That's Ghouldilocks!" replied Prince Harming. "And those are her three Scares!"

Chapter Eight
The Deal

"**Help me!**" cried Cleo as Ditto's hand began to slip from her grasp.

Resus plunged his own hand into his cape and began to rummage around for something he could use to save the changeling. If she was

caught up in the tornado, there was no knowing where she would land. First he pulled out a feather duster, then an antique bell, and finally a vacuum cleaner.

"Hurry up!" Luke urged as the faces of the three Scares melted away and then re-emerged among the chaos. Ghouldilocks was laughing now, urging the poltergeists to twirl ever faster.

"No!" bellowed Cleo as Ditto's fingers finally slid out of hers. The changeling screamed as the poltergeists lifted her higher and higher, shrieking and cackling in glee.

Quick as a flash, Prince Harming grabbed a length of rope from his belt, spun it round his head like a lasso and hurled it into the tornado. The rope twisted and buckled in the wind, but the vampire hunter was able to hold it steady enough so that as Ditto came spinning past he could pull it tight and catch her around the leg.

He pulled the rope in, hand over fist, until the little girl was within reach and he was able to stretch out and pluck her from the whirlwind. "There, there," he said. "You're OK now."

"Oh, how convenient!" thundered Resus.

"What?" shouted Luke.

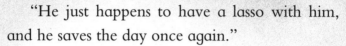

"He just happens to have a lasso with him, and he saves the day once again."

"You're mental, do you know that?" Luke exclaimed. "Now you're going to tell me Harming brought three violent poltergeists here especially to attack us!"

"Three poltergeists and the scary ghost of a girl," Resus corrected. "And he knew exactly who they were – again!"

"So he's spent a lot of time in the fairy realm."

Resus sneered. "The Crimson Queen *said* you wouldn't believe me!"

Luke stared. "You spoke to the Crimson—"

"If you two have a minute, do you think someone could possibly see their way to rescuing me?" screeched Cleo, still clinging tightly to the tree.

"All yours," said Luke, turning to Resus. "Unless, of course, Prince Harming's just biding his time until he charges in and rescues Cleo, too…"

Resus looked over at the vampire hunter, who was still trying to calm Ditto. "I can save Cleo any time I like."

Luke raised his eyebrows. "What with?" he

demanded, picking up the battery-powered vacuum cleaner. "A Dustbuster?"

"Yes, actually!" Resus barked, snatching the
vacuum cleaner from Luke's hands. He turned it
on and aimed it into the whirlwind.

The first Scare to be caught was the small-
est of them all. The baby poltergeist squealed as
it was sucked into the cleaner with a sound like
a backwards *pop!* and disappeared. The Scare
fought to get out and Resus found himself struggling to keep a grip on the handle – but he was
still smug enough to quip to Luke, "Who's been
slipping in *my* vacuum?"

"I can't believe it!" cried Luke. "It's working!"

Ghouldilocks, spotting that one of her pre-
cious Scares had been captured, let out an angry
roar.

Luke came alongside Resus and helped him
keep his grip on the cleaner as the baby ghost
inside caused it to protest. "Do you think it'll take
two more?" he yelled.

"Only one way to find out," shouted Resus,
then he flicked the power up to medium and
plunged the vacuum back into the storm. Almost
immediately, the boys captured the middle Scare,

which scrabbled around for a few seconds with transparent fingers before being sucked inside to join its sibling.

"Two down – one to go!" yelled Luke. The vampire grinned and flicked the power onto high.

The final poltergeist was the trickiest to catch. No longer restricted by the movement of its brothers, it leapt up and down as it spun around the clearing – skimming the ground one second and tearing leaves off the trees the next. The vacuum cleaner was now jerking around violently, and Luke and Resus struggled to keep control.

Ghouldilocks had become a picture of anguish. Her eyes blazed and she flung her arms around, screeching unintelligible commands to her remaining Scare.

The poltergeist shot past the boys again, but it was too fast and strong for the vacuum to have any effect.

"I've got an idea," cried Resus. "Let go!" Luke did as he was instructed and Resus charged across the patch of open ground to plunge the hoover into Ghouldilocks herself.

The result was as bizarre as it was effective. Screaming with rage, the ghoulish girl was dragged and twisted out of shape as she was sucked inside the machine. Within seconds, she was gone.

"Resus – behind you!" bellowed Luke.

Resus spun round to see the final Scare shooting through the air towards him. Standing his ground, the vampire lifted the hoover like a shotgun and simply allowed the poltergeist to slip inside. Then he switched it off, spun it around his finger and blew the last few tendrils of ectoplasmic smoke from the end of the barrel.

Cleo raced over to hug him. "That was unbelievable!" she exclaimed.

"It sure was," drawled Prince Harming. Then there was a *click!* and Resus felt the sharp point of a stake press against the side of his head.

"What do you think you're doing?" demanded Luke. "He's just saved us!"

"Yep," said Harming slowly. "He saved us all right – with items from a vampire's cloak. That ain't no costume from a school dress-up box!"

Resus swallowed hard. "But I'm *not* a vampire," he insisted, opening his mouth to show once more that he didn't have fangs.

"Then where'd you get the cloak?"

"His dad gave it to him!" Cleo blurted out. "But he's nothing like his parents – he doesn't drink blood, and he's the only kid in Scream Street who dyes his hair."

Prince Harming paused, then lowered his crossbow. "So there are real vampires in this place, Scream Street?"

Resus's eyes widened in alarm.

"No, no! I didn't mean that!" Cleo said quickly.

"Maybe you did and maybe you didn't," said Harming. "But I reckon I'll be paying this Scream Street a visit after I've dealt with the Crimson Queen."

Resus turned on Luke. "Now do you believe me? He's dangerous!"

"I'm sure it's just a mistake," Luke insisted.

86

"We can sit down and sort this out."

"You're STILL taking his side!" yelled the vampire, his eyes filling with tears. "He's just threatened to kill my parents, and you won't see him for what he is!"

Cleo took a step towards him. "Resus, I'm sorry," she sobbed. "I didn't mean to—"

"Stay away from me," Resus ordered. "All of you – just stay away! The Crimson Queen said I couldn't trust any of you, and she was right."

Luke felt a lump rise in his throat. "You were telling the truth," he gasped. "You *did* speak to the queen!"

"Oh yes," said Resus. "And she's the only one around here making any sense." He turned to face Prince Harming. "This is a real vampire cloak," he growled, "and it just happens to contain one last mirror!" He pulled a full-length mirror from his cape and stood it against a tree. The Crimson Queen was waiting patiently in its glass.

"Does the offer still stand?" Resus asked her. "If I join you, will you help me save Scream Street and turn me into a real vampire?"

"Anything you desire, Resus," replied the queen, stretching out her hand again.

With a final glance back at his friends, Resus reached into the mirror, took the queen's hand and allowed himself to be pulled through.

"Resus, no!" Cleo begged, but the vampire was now standing in the Crimson Queen's throne room. The image began to shimmer and fade, and by the time Prince Harming's stake hit the glass, all it showed was his own reflection. The mirror shattered and fell to the ground.

Chapter Nine
The Palace

"We have to stop him!" shouted Cleo, clinging tightly to the mane of Prince Harming's horse as it galloped along the path to the palace.

She and the changeling were seated in front of the vampire hunter while Luke clung on tightly behind. "We can't let him do a deal with the Crimson Queen."

"Don't you worry, little missy," said Harming. "I'll stop him, all right."

"I mean in a nice way," Cleo yelled back. "Not with sharp, pointy sticks!"

They reached the palace in no time at all. With its pale pink walls and immaculate gardens, it looked like something out of a children's picture book. Towers rose above the trees, their windows glinting in the sun, and an array of green flags flew from their tops, twisting in the breeze.

"This used to belong to the fairy royal family," said Harming as he pulled the horse back to a trot. "Until the queen made her move, that is."

"I don't get it," admitted Luke. "You said she overthrew every fairy in the land and trapped them all inside the same mirror. How is that possible?"

Harming turned round in his saddle. "Don't say you're startin' to doubt me as well?"

"Of course not," said Luke hurriedly. "It's just hard to imagine."

Prince Harming trotted the horse into the courtyard. "As hard to imagine as your best friend makin' a deal with the Queen of Darkness herself?"

He may not have been happy about what Resus had done, but Luke still bristled at the vampire hunter's words. "I'm sure he thinks he's doing what's best."

Prince Harming grunted what might have been a laugh. "All I know is that there used to be fairies aplenty around these parts, and now there ain't a single one. The realm's been handed over to monsters."

"Like Skinderella and Ghouldilocks, you mean?" said Cleo.

Harming nodded. "Them," he said, "and her…" He pointed to the palace entrance, where a young witch was cartwheeling out through the open door, accompanied by a troop of tiny men dressed in black. When they saw the newcomers, they struck aggressive poses.

"I hardly dare ask," Luke sighed. "Who are they…?"

Prince Harming unclipped his crossbow. "These folk guard the palace nowadays," he said. "Snow Fright and her seven Ninja Dwarves."

🌀 🌀 🌀

From a window high up in the palace, Resus watched the crack martial arts unit slink towards his friends. Not that they deserved to be called friends any more. Luke hadn't believed a word he'd said about that macho fraud, Prince Harming – and Cleo had practically handed his parents a death sentence.

The queen was different, though. She had led him to this awesome bedroom — his own bedroom for as long as he wanted it — before ordering the guards to attack the intruders. If only Luke and Cleo had listened to him! Then they'd have understood he was doing this for the good of everyone back home.

A fierce battle cry pulled Resus away from his thoughts and back to the scene below. The ninja dwarves backflipped across the courtyard to where Cleo, Luke and Prince Harming stood waiting.

In the background Resus could make out Ditto sitting on the vampire hunter's horse in the relative safety of the trees. If only her secret was that she could make his friends see sense! He clenched his fists as he watched the two sides prepare to fight, his fake fingernails digging sharply into the palms of his hands. He hoped no one would get hurt, despite what they'd—

"There you are!"

Resus spun round to see the Crimson Queen entering the room. She was even more beautiful in real life, and he caught himself wondering if she was shrouded in an enchantment charm like Eefa and her sister back home.

"No," smiled the queen. "No enchantment charm."

Resus swallowed hard. He'd have to get used to the queen being able to read his thoughts. "I was, er … just coming to find you," he said.

"Of course you were. But first you wanted to check on your friends."

"They're no friends of mine," muttered Resus.

"Now, now," the queen scolded. "Just because they don't see things as clearly as us doesn't mean they don't have good hearts. It's simply time for you to follow a different path."

"About that," said Resus. "When can you make me a real vampire? And when can we get rid of the normals from Scream Street and close the doorway?"

"All in good time, my dear. All in good time…"

Resus could hear war cries and the clash of weapons from the courtyard below. The fight had begun, and he wished he had the nerve to turn round to see if Luke and Cleo were OK. "It's just that…"

The Crimson Queen pressed a perfectly mani-cured finger to his lips as the door opened behind

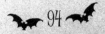

her. A girl entered the room – but she was not like any girl Resus had seen before. She appeared to be made of wood, and instead of legs and feet she had long, rippling roots that trailed along behind her.

"Don't be alarmed!" the queen giggled at Resus's look of astonishment. "This is just one of my Creeping Beauties!"

The girl bowed gently, creaking like an old oak door. She handed the queen a set of new clothes.

"These are for you," announced the queen, giving them to Resus. "Put them on and be in my throne room in five minutes." Then she turned and swept back out through the door followed by her silent wooden handmaiden.

Resus waited until he heard the door click shut, then he threw the suit over a chair and turned back to peer out of the window at the action below.

The dwarf named Ugly roared with anger and rushed at Luke only to find himself being lifted off the ground by his collar. His legs kicked wildly as he struggled to get free. "This fight doesn't feel fair," commented Luke, tossing the dwarf into the nearby fountain. "It's like we're beating up some little kids at school."

"We didn't have children like this in my classes back in Egypt," said Cleo, gripping Puky's arm and spinning him round. The dwarf flushed a disturbing shade of green. "If you're sick on my bandages, I'll feed you to Skinderella!" snapped Cleo as she let the tiny figure go. Pukey raced away through the bushes, a hand clamped over his mouth.

It was true to say, the battle wasn't going Snow Fright's way. Her ninja dwarves were obviously only used to fighting creatures their own size, not those that could easily pick them up and throw them aside. The witch herself, having realized that her crack squad of martial artists was being beaten, had turned herself into a rosy red apple and now sat silently on the palace steps.

Prince Harming sported a leather whip, and with a flick of his wrist managed to snare Pensive and tie him up with it. The dwarf snarled as the vampire hunter snatched up the apple and wedged it between his little teeth.

Beery staggered towards Luke, downing the last of a bottle of Hakeley's Old Abrasive ale.

Tossing the bottle aside, he burped loudly, sang a verse of an utterly unintelligible song, then passed out on the grass.

"How many more are there?" asked Luke, stepping over the snoring figure to push Ugly back into the fountain as he struggled to climb out of the water.

"I'm not sure," said Cleo, giving Wonky a kick up the backside and sending him scuttling away, crying. "They won't stand still long enough for me to count them."

Luke hoisted up Aerodynamic and hurled him into the nearest bush. Then, aside from the odd dwarvish groan of pain, the courtyard fell silent.

"Look!" hissed Cleo, pointing at a window high above them. Resus quickly ducked out of sight.

"At least we know where he is," said Luke.

Cleo nodded. "Let's fetch Ditto and get up there." As she made her way over to where the horse and changeling were patiently waiting, she suddenly spotted Prince Harming slumped against a statue of a fairy. A large bruise was spreading across his forehead.

"Are you OK?" she asked, hurrying over.

"I'll be fine," drawled the vampire hunter. "I just took a clobberin' from old Thumpy – but he came off worse." As if to illustrate his point, he pulled the drowsy dwarf out from behind the statue and used him to mop his brow. "You two go find your friend."

Cleo frowned. "But you said he was nothing but a low-down vampire…"

Prince Harming laughed. "Don't pay no attention to me, little lady. He ain't no vampire – least not till the Crimson Queen gets him in her clutches. Now get up there and show him who his real friends are! He don't… He…" The vampire hunter's words faded to nothing as he fell back, unconscious.

Luke turned to Cleo. "He's right," he said.

"We can't just leave him here," protested Cleo. He's unconsious!"

"Which means he can't get into any trouble," said Luke. "And he's pretty much out of sight here. We can come back for him once we've found Resus and Poppy – although I've no idea how we're going to get up there."

"Leave that to me," smiled Cleo. "I've *bean*

99

waiting for a chance to use this." She produced the magic bean from their lesson that morning and tossed it into the fountain. Immediately it began to sprout both roots and a stem – which grew and grew, taller and thicker, until within seconds it had become a fully fledged beanstalk, soon reaching the top of the palace.

Cleo gestured for Luke to take the first step onto the beanstalk. "After you," she grinned, lifting Ditto onto her back.

And they began to climb.

Chapter Ten
The Mirror

When Resus entered the queen's throne room, he was dressed more finely than ever before. The red suit he had been given was made of the finest silk, and it fitted him perfectly. His hair was slicked back, and he wore a brand new pair of hand-crafted leather shoes. The outfit was made complete by a long, red vampire cape that swished around his ankles as he walked.

Several Creeping Beauties surrounded the queen's throne, talking to their mistress in hushed whispers. Resus didn't quite know what to do. Should he let them know he had arrived, or just wait until they noticed him? He chose the latter, and spotting a mirror hanging at the far end of the room he decided to head over and check out his new look.

Stopping in front of the mirror, he froze. Instead of a well-dressed young vampire staring back at him, there were dozens – no, hundreds – of men, women and children crammed together behind the glass. Each wore a tutu and sported a pair of tiny wings. The fairies! Prince Harming had been right – the Crimson Queen had captured every fairy in the realm and now kept them captive in her magic mirror.

Resus moved closer to the mirror. It was clear the fairies could see him, because their mouths were moving as though they were calling to him – but no sound escaped. The fairies at the front hammered their fists against the glass, pleading with Resus to set them free.

"Beautiful, isn't it?"

Resus jumped. The Crimson Queen was standing right behind him.

"It's, er…" Resus struggled to keep his mind blank and not think about the horror and disgust he felt at the fairies' imprisonment. "It's different," he mumbled finally. "My mum and dad just have a family portrait hanging over our fireplace."

The queen threw back her head and laughed. "You and I are going to get along just fine, Resus!" She smiled at him. "It's the start of a new life for all three of us."

Resus frowned. "*Three* of us?" He felt something tugging at his trousers and looked down to see Poppy gazing up at him, sucking her thumb. She was dressed in a pretty pink party frock.

"Poppy!" he cried, sweeping the toddler up into his arms and hugging her tightly. "Thank goodness you're safe!" He turned back to the queen. "I thought you didn't want to keep her."

"I don't," the queen said coldly. "But as there are no other children here, I thought she might prove company for you."

"Until I go back to Scream Street," Resus reminded her.

 103

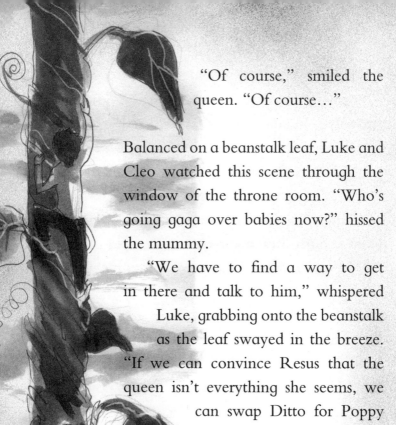

"Of course," smiled the queen. "Of course…"

Balanced on a beanstalk leaf, Luke and Cleo watched this scene through the window of the throne room. "Who's going gaga over babies now?" hissed the mummy.

"We have to find a way to get in there and talk to him," whispered Luke, grabbing onto the beanstalk as the leaf swayed in the breeze. "If we can convince Resus that the queen isn't everything she seems, we can swap Ditto for Poppy and all go home."

"No," said Cleo flatly. "We're not leaving Ditto behind."

"What?" cried Luke. "You can't say that! We've come all this way to swap the changeling for Eefa's niece, and now you don't want to?"

"Ditto is terrified of the queen!" said Cleo. "There's no way we're leaving her here." The changeling already had her face buried in Cleo's shoulder and she was trembling.

"Then what do we do with her?" asked Luke.

"We take her back with us. She can come and live with me."

"But she came from the fairy realm," Luke pointed out. "She belongs here."

"No, she doesn't," Cleo retorted. "No one belongs here with that wicked woman, least of all a little—"

Suddenly, the throne room window swung open. "Are you sure you wouldn't be more comfortable indoors?" asked the Crimson Queen.

Resus stared at his friends, now held fast in the branch-like arms of two Creeping Beauties. A third had taken Poppy and Ditto off to play together in the vampire's bedroom.

"You have to help us!" Cleo begged, struggling against the sinister, woody creature.

Resus took a nervous step forward, but the queen laid her hand on his arm. "I... I can't," he croaked. "The queen is going to make me a real vampire and help to save Scream Street. We'll

get rid of the normals once and for all."

"She's filling you full of lies!" Luke shouted. "Just look at that mirror! She's trapped every fairy from the entire realm in there! That's why Twinkle was too scared to come near the place – she'd have captured him, too!"

"The queen has told me why she had to do that," Resus said. "The fairies were taking over – making life difficult for the people who lived here before. It's just like the normals and Scream Street."

Cleo frowned. "So you'd imprison all the normals in a magic mirror just to put things back to how they used to be at home?"

Resus nodded defiantly. "If I had to."

The Crimson Queen sat on her throne, enjoying the heated exchange between the three friends. She reached down to a basket at her side and took out a cake.

"Resus, this isn't you," said Luke. "You're not like her."

"No, Luke," Resus retorted. "I'm exactly like her. I'm a vampire!"

He was shocked to see Luke smile at his words. "You still think she's a real vampire?"

The Crimson Queen leapt up from her throne. "Quiet!" she commanded.

Resus turned to her. "What's he talking about?"

"He's trying to trick you," said the queen. "Leave this to me and run along to your room. We can have dinner together later."

"Don't listen to her!" cried Luke. "Look into her eyes. She's scared."

The queen stalked across the throne room to where Luke was still being held tightly by the Creeping Beauty. "What makes you say that?" she hissed.

"Because I know who you really are," said Luke confidently.

"What are you talking about?" asked Cleo in surprise.

"I've worked it out," replied Luke. "She—"

"Silence!" roared the queen.

"I don't think so," said Luke determinedly. "Now, why don't you toddle off and have another cake?"

"I still don't get it," said Cleo.

"Think about it," said Luke. "Skinderella, Ghouldilocks, Snow Fright… They're all scary versions of characters from well-known fairy tales." He stared up into the blazing eyes of the queen. "This one's no exception. She's no *Crimson Queen* – she's Little Red Riding Hood!"

The queen sneered, baring her fangs. "You mean Little Red Riding *Blood*!"

"Call yourself whatever you like," Luke said. "You're still a dark fairy … and you're still scared of me."

The Crimson Queen laughed mockingly. "And why would I be scared of you, little boy?"

Luke looked straight at her with a steely glint in his eye. "Because I'm the Big Bad Wolf!"

Resus and Cleo had never seen Luke transform so fast. He roared as his bones began to reshape and his muscles stretched and knotted into their werewolf configurations. By the time the thick brown fur had sprouted over every inch of his body, his claws and fangs had already ripped through his skin. With a single sweep of his powerful paw, Luke's werewolf sent his captor crashing to the floor.

Growling deep in his throat, the werewolf stalked towards the Crimson Queen.

"R–Resus!" she croaked, backing away. "In

my cake basket, you'll find a dagger. Take it and kill the wolf!"

Resus looked over at the basket sitting on the floor beside the throne. He could just see the handle of the dagger sticking out from beneath a checked tablecloth. He hesitated.

"If you ever want to become a real vampire, kill him!" screamed the queen as Luke slunk closer.

Resus reached into the basket and retrieved the dagger. It felt heavy and awkward in his hand.

"NO!" screamed Cleo. "Don't do it!"

The queen could feel the werewolf's breath on her face. "Kill him, now!"

Resus stared at the knife in his hand. "Never," he breathed.

The queen tripped and fell. Luke's werewolf stood over her, saliva dripping from his powerful jaws.

"Admit defeat and we'll call him off," shouted Cleo from the other end of the room. "It's all over!"

The Crimson Queen's eyes flicked away from the wolf's and looked over his shoulder. She smiled. "It's nowhere near over," she said. "You're forgetting what happens in my story..."

"What are you going to do?" said Cleo. "Set your grandmother on us?"

"Not quite," drawled Prince Harming, entering the room, a large axe gripped in his fists. "Maybe the woodcutter will do."

"You!" snapped Resus, still holding tightly to the queen's dagger.

The werewolf turned and snarled at Harming as he strode into the room. "You were right to choose him, Your Majesty," said the woodcutter, nodding towards Resus and reaching out to help the Crimson Queen to her feet. "He's smart – the only one to spot that I'd set up the attacks in the forest – but too weak to convince his friends."

The werewolf lifted its snout in the air and howled angrily.

"It's been quite an adventure," said Prince Harming. He raised his axe and aimed it at Luke.

"Such a shame it has to end this way…"

"Please, no!" cried Cleo.

"Say goodbye, little doggy," snarled Harming.

"STOP!" yelled Resus. Both the Crimson Queen and the vampire hunter looked over to see him pointing the dagger at them, his hands shaking.

"Ignore him," the queen commanded. "He hasn't got the nerve to kill anyone."

"You're right," said Resus. "I haven't." Then he turned and threw the dagger directly at the magic mirror.

Chapter Eleven
The Rescue

As the mirror smashed, the throne room began to buzz with the sound of a thousand wings. The fairies were finally free.

One of the larger fairies – an elderly man with ragged, grey hair – barked orders to the younger ones around him. They nodded and quickly surrounded the Crimson Queen and Prince Harming, relieving them of their weapons. Other fairies soared across the room to free Cleo from her Creeping Beauty.

"Where is the changeling?" asked the old fairy, scanning the room.

"They took her to another room, with Poppy," replied Resus. "I know where it is." With that he dashed out of the room, two fairies in tow.

Suddenly there was a snarl from the corner of the room. Luke's werewolf, clearly startled by the newcomers, had backed into a corner and was growling angrily. A young fairy drew a magic wand from the waistband of his tutu.

"No!" cried Cleo, hurrying over to the wolf. "He's one of us – and he's just scared. He doesn't think like a human when he's in this form."

The fairy hovered over to Cleo and smiled. "We saw everything," he assured her. "We wish him no harm – but I must protect our brethren from his animal instincts." He waved the wand and a large bubble appeared around Luke's

 113

werewolf, causing him to look eerily like a large hamster in a ball. "We can cancel the spell once your friend reverts to human form," the fairy smiled.

"Get your hands off me!" Cleo turned to see two fairies holding the Crimson Queen firmly by the arms. Meanwhile, Prince Harming was being pinned down by another four.

The elderly fairy flapped over to the queen. "Hello again, Red," he said.

"Fennel!" spat the queen. "How lovely to see you again!"

"Is it true?" Cleo asked him. "Is she really a dark fairy?"

Fennel nodded. "One of such power as has not been witnessed for an age."

"But I know the story of Little Red Riding Hood," said Cleo. "And I don't remember her being a vampire – even a pretend one!"

"Tales of the dark folk have been told for generations," Fennel explained. "Mostly as a

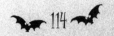

warning to others. It is not impossible for embellishments and changes to have occurred over the centuries." He turned to face the room. "In fact, I believe the latest version of Snow Fright's tale has her dwarves setting off for work each morning in a diamond mine!" The other fairies laughed at the idea.

"So, what will you do with her?" asked Cleo.

Fennel sighed. "Alas, I do not know," he admitted. "I would suggest a similar punishment to that which she inflicted upon us — imprisonment in a magic mirror. But there are no mirrors left in the fairy realm. The queen had them all smashed in case we found a way to travel from one to another after she sealed us in."

"That's where you're wrong," declared Resus, re-entering the throne room dressed in his own clothes again. Two fairies flew in behind him, each carrying one of the little girls.

"I thought you used your final mirror back in the woods?" said Cleo.

"I did," grinned Resus. "But luckily I'm not the only one who's vain!" Stepping over to Prince Harming, he reached into the vampire hunter's pocket and pulled out the battered old hand mirror.

"Perfect," said Fennel. He took the mirror from Resus and pulled out his magic wand.

"No!" screamed the queen. "You can't do this to me!"

"I'm not just doing it to you," said the fairy. "I'm doing it to both of you…"

Prince Harming finally found his tongue. "What?" he cried. "No! Don't put me in there with her! I'll do anything, just lock me up by myself! Please!"

Fennel cast his spell and there was a flash of white sparkles. When they cleared, the Crimson Queen and Prince Harming were both squashed up against the glass of the tiny mirror. "Now," said the fairy, "let's find a nice, safe place to put this where it won't be disturbed."

"I can't believe it's all over," said Cleo, hugging both Ditto and Poppy.

"Er … excuse me!" They all turned to see Luke, now back in human form, rolling towards them inside his giant bubble. "What's going on?"

Luke and Resus climbed through the new Hex Hatch straight from the throne room and into the garden of 27 Scream Street. Cleo followed,

holding a small, blonde toddler by the hand.

"Poppy!" Luella cried. She raced across the garden to hug her daughter. "Thank you so much!" she cried.

"Our pleasure," Luke smiled. "We were happy to help."

"You might not be too happy when you hear our news," said Eefa. "We haven't been able to break the spell sealing Femur's tomb."

"So we still can't get in?" asked Cleo.

"I'm sorry," said Eefa, shaking her head. "The magic is just too strong for us."

"But not, perhaps, for us?" suggested Fennel, flying in through the Hex Hatch behind them, Ditto in his arms. Eefa and Luella stared in amazement as a dozen more fairies appeared behind him.

"You wanted to know what this little one's secret is," said Fennel, landing gently beside the group.

"That's right," replied Cleo, "but we couldn't work it out."

Fennel's eyes sparkled. "Then watch…" He put Ditto down on the grass and waved his magic wand over her. There was another burst of white

sparkles and, suddenly, a beautiful fairy dressed in a glistening silver robe was standing in the changeling's place. The other fairies all dropped to one knee and bowed their heads.

"What's going on?" asked Luke.

"I'm the Fairy Godmother," explained the silver fairy. "The true Queen of the Fairy Realm."

"But a minute ago you were just an annoying – er, I mean … a changeling," gasped Resus.

"That is what we hoped you would believe," the Fairy Godmother smiled.

Luke's eyes widened. "So you took Poppy's

place and sent her to the palace in the fairy realm?"

"We had no choice," said the Fairy Godmother. "We didn't have enough power to escape Little Red's imprisonment, but by combining our magic, the fairies were just able to disguise me and make the switch in the hope of attracting rescuers from outside our world."

"That's a heck of a secret!" said Resus. "I always thought it would be something like the ability to burp a selection of nursery rhymes."

"I can do that, too," said the fairy queen with a wink, "but we'll save it for another day…"

"Can you help us?" Luke asked her. "Can you break the spell surrounding the tomb?"

"I shall certainly try," replied the Fairy Godmother, producing a silver magic wand. She waved it in front of the tomb, and to the children's delight, the stone door instantly slid open.

"You did it!" cried Cleo.

"Thank you so much!" said Luke.

"It's nothing compared to how you have helped my people," smiled the Fairy Godmother. "We are the ones who should thank you." Then she flapped her wings, rose up in the air and

flew back into her own realm, her subjects close behind.

Once the fairies had left Scream Street and the Hex Hatch had closed behind them, Resus took Femur's skull from his cloak. "Go on, then," he said, handing the relic to Luke.

"No," replied Luke. "This one we all do together." So he, Resus and Cleo stepped inside the tomb and placed the skull at the top of the skeleton lying inside.

"Did it work?" asked Femur Ribs, sitting up.

Screams could be heard in the central square as the green section of the doorway to Luke's world exploded in a shower of sparks, shrinking the entrance. "It certainly sounds like it," grinned Cleo. "Thank you, Femur!"

"My pleasure," replied the skeleton. "Now – let's go and see the fun."

The trio helped their friend to her feet and dashed back out into the garden to catch the last of the emerald fireworks as they exploded in the afternoon sky.

"Only one more relic to give back," grinned Luke, putting an arm around each of his friends.

"Which might be difficult from where you're

going," gurgled an unfamiliar voice.

Before the trio could see who had spoken, Luke was pulled roughly away from Resus and Cleo, and a pair of handcuffs was slipped over his wrists and locked. He looked up to find himself surrounded by Movers in brown jumpsuits.

Luke paled. "What are you doing?" he yelled, tugging at the handcuffs.

A man with green, scaly skin stepped into view. He wore a smart business suit, which appeared to be soaked with water. "Don't struggle," he glugged, gills at the sides of his throat flapping. "It will only make things worse for you and your friends."

Luke looked around and saw that Resus and Cleo had also been captured. "Who are you?" he demanded.

"My name is Acrid Belcher," replied the man. "Head of the Government Housing Of Unusual Life-forms − or G.H.O.U.L., as you youngsters like to call it."

Resus took a deep breath. "This isn't good…"

"No, Master Negative, it isn't," spat Belcher, water dribbling from his thick, rubbery lips. "This isn't good at all! You are under arrest for opening

 121

a doorway to another world and allowing normals to enter Scream Street!"

"We only did the doorway bit," cried Cleo. "It was Sir Otto Sneer who brought the normals in!"

"And a profitable little venture it's been, too," laughed the landlord, entering the garden at that very moment. "Here you go, Belcher, my old mucker," he said, handing the slippery green man a wedge of money. "Your cut from this week's takings."

"They're in it together!" Resus exclaimed.

Sir Otto plucked his cigar out of his mouth. "Who'd have thought I'd finally meet a freak I get along with – and a slime beast, at that!"

Luke glared up at him. "I suppose it's too much to hope that you're really Zeal Chillchase in disguise."

The landlord bit down on his cigar and stroked the white silk scarf around his neck. "Tough luck, kid."

"Zeal Chillchase no longer works for G.H.O.U.L.," bubbled Acrid Belcher. "Once his role in this fiasco was uncovered, he was punished."

"What have you done to him?" demanded Cleo.

Belcher smiled, and as he did so his gills stretched out alarmingly. "The same as I plan to do to you."

"Our parents won't let you get away with this," Luke growled at the slime beast. "Someone will tell them and they'll put a stop to it."

"On the contrary, I will tell them myself!" snarled Belcher. "Your parents will be coming with us to G.H.O.U.L. headquarters. After all, it would be very boring if there was no one there to watch me pass sentence." He turned to the nearest Mover and placed a wet, slimy hand against his forehead. "Take the prisoners away!" he ordered.

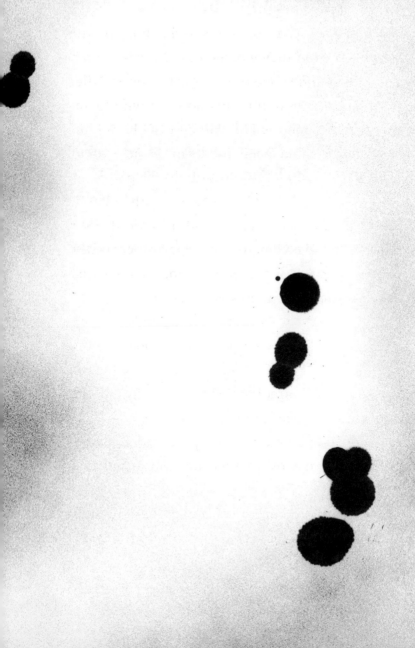

Epilogue

Mr and Mrs Watson gripped the bars of the viewing area as they watched the Movers march Luke, Resus and Cleo over to the trapdoor. Niles Farr and Resus's mum and dad were with them. The trip through the Hex Hatch to G.H.O.U.L. headquarters had been made in silence, apart from the occasional sob from Bella Negative.

The trio had their hands tied and they stood, staring miserably at their parents as Acrid Belcher approached, clutching a roll of parchment. Cleo began to shake. Resus fought back tears as he caught sight of his mum's stricken face.

"Defendants," the slime beast gurgled. "You have been charged with opening a magical doorway out of a G.H.O.U.L. community, allowing thousands of normals to enter and disrupt the lives of its residents. Do you deny these charges?"

"You don't understand," protested Luke. "I just wanted a way to take my mum and dad home…"

"Then you admit to collecting the six founding fathers' relics and using their power to open a doorway back to your old world?"

"Yes, but—"

"Enough!" barked Belcher. "You are guilty of the charges brought against you, and sentence will now be passed."

Luke gulped and didn't say any more.

"Luke Watson, Resus Negative, Cleo Farr – you will now be banished to the Underlands for the rest of your natural lives, however long that might be."

Acrid Belcher grasped the lever beside him and pulled it back hard. The trapdoor swung open with a barely audible creak, plunging Luke, Resus and Cleo into the dark, swirling abyss beneath…

Tommy Donbavand was born and brought up in Liverpool and has worked at numerous careers, including actor, theatre producer, children's entertainer, clown (called Wobblebottom), drama teacher and writer. His non-fiction books for children and their parents, such as *Boredom Busters* and *Quick Fixes for Bored Kids*, helped him to become a regular guest on radio stations around the UK and he also writes for a number of magazines, including *Creative Steps* and Scholastic's *Junior Education*.

Tommy says the idea for comedy-horror series *Scream Street* came from wondering what it would be like to live in a haunted house – and to have another haunted house next door. Before long he had invented a whole street of horrific homes and populated this nightmarish neighbourhood with every kind of scary creature he could imagine.

When he's not writing, Tommy likes to make balloon animals and play the harmonica – and he dreams of the day when he'll be able to do both at the same time.

www.tommydonbavand.com

www.screamstreet.co.uk